Praise for Ron Collins

"Ron Collins is a master of short fiction"

Kristine Kathryn Rusch
Hugo Award-Winning Series Editor, *Fiction River*

First Rays of New Sun

A Short Story

Ron Collins

SKYFOX
PUBLISHING
Fantasy

Contents

For the genre-bender in each of us

First Rays of New Sun

"Katazarra," Hadroc said as he came into the library, "I need you to take care of James."

I set my book on the stand beside my upholstered chair, noting the golden glow the soft daylight gave as if fell over the exposed skin of my shoulder. The cold remains of my tea had long ago filled the crevasses of the room with its flavor. From outside the window came muted voices and the clatterings of preparation for tonight's festival.

Hadroc came to a halt, his silk-lined cape swirling to a rest.

He was a beautiful man—angular and tall in the way of all fae, but even more fair and more angular than the rest. The musk of soil and harsh-cut wood surged at his entrance, scents that were mixed with the unmistakable odor of recent sex. His cheekbones were flush. The gaze of his eyes —which could be beautiful one moment, then freeze to daggers the next—was crystalline and watery now. As always occurred, I shuddered with memories of his body as soon as I laid eyes on him: the strength of his arms, the hardness of the muscles along his back. I remembered the feeling of his fingers pressing into the low slope of my backbone.

Even now, after everything, I felt pulled to him.

That is the nature of fairy magic. Hadroc's hold is as bold and wonderful as it is terrifying and everlasting.

"I assume, then, that this must be James," I replied, examining the man who followed Hadroc.

I might have considered him to be stunning also if it weren't for the nearness of Hadroc. The human was the flipside of the fae lord, dark complexioned with a shock of black hair falling over his forehead. His sharp-edged cheekbones underscored eyes so dark that irises melted seamlessly into black pupils. James was as thin as Hadroc, too, but where the fae's movements were smooth and pure, James's were awkward and abrupt, made as if his mortal brain continually interrupted them to consider some other action. He wore human clothes as well as a human aura—hiking apparel, mostly, denim dungarees and a flannel shirt, both of which had certainly been removed earlier, but now had been returned to cover James's toned body.

His fear was palpable under a forced stoicism.

His bootsteps were heavy on the hardwood floor.

"I am needed at the construction," Hadroc said. "And I need James to have a partner for lunch."

"I see," I replied.

Those words, combined with the undercurrent of annoyance in the fae's gaze were enough to tell the tale. James had fallen for the fae, as will most humans Hadroc desires. But unlike most, James was conversant with lore. He understood that to take food in the land of fairy would bind him to Hadroc forever, and that wasn't on his agenda. Hadroc was in command of the preparations for Alban Arthan, the forthcoming Winterfest celebration that would draw the old year to its end and see the birth of the new. There would be dancing and music, much wine and, of course, much of all the other frivolities that came with dance, music, and wine. It was the highlight of the fae year.

Hadroc's position meant he had a built-in excuse for his departure, but the years had been long for me and I knew he was more inconvenienced in this matter than he was over-worked. Rather than do the dirty work himself, the fae lord wanted me to find a way to get the young man to eat. The edge to his watery gaze also said that the punishment for failing him would be severe.

Severe for Hadroc, as I already understood, was not a trifling thing.

I stood and ran my hand down the velour side panels on my dress, mostly to remove wrinkles that had come from my time seated though I cannot lie about my desire to see a moment of hunger on Hadroc's gaze. The garment was well fitted, and the fae are nothing if not transparent in their admiration of beauty over certain other qualities.

"I'm sure I can keep James entertained," I said, drawing the approval from Hadroc I craved.

"That's wonderful, love," he said.

My heart clenched as Hadroc breezed out of the room.

The silence he left behind was as if the entire place took a collective sigh, then, thankfully, the distant crash of an axe cleaving wood broke the moment.

I drew a breath and glanced to James.

His eyes drew half-closed as he appraised me in ways he hadn't while Hadroc was here. Without thinking, I found myself presenting an angle that would let the dress do its work. A moment later I lifted my hand toward James, palm down.

"Come, come," I said, beckoning with a glint to my eye that I knew would convince any who were not fae.

"I'm not hungry," James said, clearly in control of himself now.

"You may not desire food," I said. "But I have my orders, and you can save me no little trouble by at least accompanying me while I partake."

His smile was as abrupt as if I had interrupted him.

"I can understand that," he said.

I turned my hand over, still extending it. This time he took it.

His grip was smoother than I would have guessed from his outdoorsy attire. His fingers were as strong as Hadroc's. His hand was firm and warm.

I understand what Hadroc saw in him, I thought as I led him from the library, through the hall, and toward the kitchen.

The building was a huge network of chambers and passages built under and around the canopy of the great expanse of Fairyland forest over the years. Wings of the manor serve both as Hadroc's living quarters and the place where he conducts his business, whatever that is at the moment. Like most fae, his interests shift like tides along the oceanfront.

James spent the trip looking at the place as if he was seeing it for the first time, which I suppose is true enough. I'm certain that he's not been out of Hadroc's, uh, sight since coming to Fairy, until now, and as long as Hadroc is in a room the glamour he emits will absorb all attentions.

Seeing wonder on the face of new arrivals is the only part of my role that I liked, so I watched as we progressed past the arched goldenwood of the central hallway, and traversed the simple passage of stairways that led to the working areas of the center. His gaze was like a squirrel in a tree, skittering from limb to limb in short bursts, landing, hesitating with nervous anticipation, then moving again.

The kitchen and dining centers are on the third level of a backhouse. The sweet smells of cold meats and fresh fruits stirred my stomach as we approached.

I took a plate and filled it with more than I could eat.

James remained emptyhanded, which I allowed.

"This is an amazing place," James said.

"Yes," I replied. "I call it the Tree Castle."

He gave the desired chuckle. "I see why."

We took a seat at an ornate table of carved oak that sat on the open patio. It gave us a view that looked over the forest to the north and the open grounds where the dancing would be held later tonight to the east. The manor yard's magicked grass was vivid green against the dead of winter around it.

At this height the forest felt like a tapestry of leafless branches.

The dry air was cold, and blowing hard enough that it threw James's dark hair back from his head, but fires at each corner of the space kept the table warm enough.

Below, fae folk worked on the grounds, without, of course, any help from or even sighting of Hadroc. A set of three podiums had been constructed at equidistant points around the open glade, each large enough to hold a band of musicians when the event began. Evergreen and holy-spruce ringed the area as if it were a protective fence against the press of oak and birch that filled the forest around us. Every door in sight was adorned with arrangements of holly or mistletoe. Unfurled banners rolled from the sills of every window, adorned with the fertility symbols of goats and lions.

"I like it outside," I said, taking in the sky as we sat. "It makes me feel like the world is limitless."

I slid my plate to the space between us, hoping the pure nearness of faeland nourishment would sway his senses, but he was resolute. Undaunted, I selected an apricot. Its flesh was coarse and tasted sweet on my tongue.

"How long have you been here?" James asked.

"Time is hard to track in Fairy," I replied, knowing I could tell him the exact passage, but that he would find the answer annoying. "Besides, clocks move differently here."

"When were you taken?"

"The year I last remember was 2026."

James's lips curled upward and a crease came to the corner of his eyes. He nodded with a motion that was hard to interpret. He looked at me with an unnerving calm.

"Do you like apricots?" I said to deflect my anxiety.

"No."

"Then maybe you should try the turkey. It's fresh and straight from the heart of Fairyland. Beyond belief."

"I'm sure it is."

My suggestions did nothing to bring food closer to his lips, nor did it dampen the inquisitive edge to his expression.

"I'm sure it's been ages since you last ate," I said, thinking pragmatism might win out. "And given your recent activities you've got to be starving-hungry by now. You might as well eat something. You won't be allowed to leave either way."

"We'll see."

I ate in silence for several moments, absorbing the nature of James's temperament.

He examined the area with the eye of a surveyor.

I put myself in James's position and assessed the Tree Castle as if I were not enthralled, looking for paths to escape if such a thing had been possible, but finding the drop to the forest floor too far, the nettled branches of the treescape too dense, and the guarded perimeters too well staffed.

The food was suddenly less flavorful.

Gently, James reached across the table and ran a finger down my jawbone.

I let him.

The caress was light, just the tip of one finger. I thought about where that finger had been earlier this morning, imagined it caressing Hadroc's jaw, tracing a path down the fae lord's neck to his chest and then the soft hairs that lined the smooth skin on Hadroc's belly.

Then the sensation was gone and I was left with nothing but an empty form of jealousy.

"You're an artificial life," he said, pulling his hand back. "A robot."

"You can tell?"

"It's not hard when you know exactly what you're looking for. You're an older model."

My face must have darkened.

"I'm sorry if that hurt you."

"It's all right."

"How did you wind up here?"

"Same way you did," I said with a sharpness that gave me back the sense of self I had temporarily fumbled. "I gave in to Hadroc."

He frowned.

"That doesn't make sense."

"You'd best get used to it," I replied with a wry chuckle at the quaint sense of betrayal he showed. "When it comes to beautiful creatures and sex, you'll find Hadroc isn't particularly discerning when it comes to gender."

He blushed. "That's not what I meant."

"Then what did you mean?"

"I meant you're not human."

I glared at him, fighting an automatic response to an old prejudice. "If you're trying to be less offensive, you're failing miserably."

"I mean...."

"We have to eat, too, you know?"

"Yeah, I get it. Eat the food here, and you're caught. But while you eat to be more humanlike, you're still not human."

"I convert food energy to fill my batteries, or I die."

"Of course you do," he snapped.

I peered at him. If form held, then Hadroc had picked him up in a hard-pounding bar someplace in the middle of a metropolis. But his questions made me wonder about him. Was there something more here than the usual? Something in James's appearance here beyond a random hookup with a deliriously beautiful fae lord?

Where was he from? What was he doing here?

"So I'm not human," I said, pushing the idea away for now. I had a job to complete, and I intended to do it. "What of it?"

"How does fae magic work on a robot?" he said.

"How does it work on a human?"

"That's not the point."

"Yes it is," I said, an old, more familiar anger rising. "That is *exactly* the point. It's always been *exactly* the point." I stood up and the chair juddered over the slats of the patio floor as I felt heat surge through my spine to crash over the rest of my body. Other fae in the area stared. "I may be out of my time phase, James, but even when I was in your realm I understood the fact that I had my autonomy. And I understood that people like you would do whatever you could to take it away."

I stomped off, then, feeling the glorious release of pent-up frustration tingling all the way to my fingertips.

Let him starve, I thought as I stomped through the Tree Castle and out into the chill of winter.

Hadroc would be upset if he found out, but I had had enough.

I t was several minutes later before that feeling faded. The woods were empty on this, the shortest, coldest day of the year.

I had chosen my boots for their fashion with my dress, but they were comfortable, too, as most fae footwork will be. They crushed dry leaves and crinkled peat moss as I rushed through the evergreen barrier and entered the wooded expanse. I ran further, wanting to be away. The conversation with James had brought up sour thoughts that laid across my already sour sensations about being alone for so long.

The call of a solitary owl echoed in the space between my steps.

Though the air was crystalline sharp, it smelled of barren soil and future snow.

I adjusted my inner works to raise my temperature, expelling bursts of breath in cloudy plumes as I went, knowing those breaths brought me oxygen I craved just as surely as they brought humans the oxygen they needed, oxygen that helped the fleshy portions of my body grow and that made me who I was as much as the code and networks that ran the core of my body's operations did.

As I ran, elements of anger gave way to the feeling of a certain joy that I hadn't felt for too long.

Too long cooped up in the Tree Castle.

Too long reading and sleeping, talking to the staff, and, occasionally, far too rarely, accepting the visitations of the fae lord who had enthralled me so many years ago.

How long had it been?

I stopped my running and leaned on an ancient oak. Its bark was thick and corky to my fingers. I put my forehead against it, remembering the first time.

Hadroc had captured Alonzo, a human who was technically my sponsor—the man who, by the new human laws, agreed to vouch for my behavior, effectively cosigning a loan on my freedom and giving me the autonomy so many humans take for granted. Alonzo and I were together that night, dancing at the Car-a-Go nightclub, a place like others I now know Hadroc patrols. Alonzo saw him. Hadroc did his fae thing, and things led to things.

It was fun.

We woke up in the place I came to know as the Tree Castle.

Alonzo was famished. How was he to know? Hadroc left him a plate on the nightstand, and he ate it before anyone could suggest otherwise.

I remember Alonzo begging, grasping Hadroc's hand.

"Please," he said. "I have so much to do."

Hadroc's lips curled in the sympathetic manner he has, his eyes softening in a way that makes you think he's going to give you what you need. "I love you too much to give you back," he said.

I remembered Alonzo turning to me, perplexion on his face.

Heavy footsteps behind me broke the spell of my ruminations.

James crashed through the forest, panting, the cold air bringing a ruddy glow to his skin that served to heighten his ruggedness. I was not without my urges, and it had been a while since Hadroc's last visit. I am not of a mind to hide myself from the truth, no matter how painful it might be. At that moment, James carried a sense of hero with him that made me stir. I remembered the firmness of his grip while we were in the library, paired with the softness of his hands. My distaste for the image brought me confusion. Where did this desire come from? Was it lust of the heart, or a piece of code dropped somewhere in a register of my memories and processors?

Did I really want to know?

He stopped several arm distances away.

The forest seemed to shrink to the span of this tiny clearing, and the breeze settled to stillness. The chill was still strong enough, though, that I worried that the thin flannel of his shirt would not keep away the pneumonia. Humans have weaknesses that artificial life forms do not.

"Don't run," he said, already gathering his composure from the exertion.

"Who are you?" I said.

"I'm just a guy."

"Don't lie to me."

His self-congratulatory smile gave him away.

"Your meeting with Hadroc was no accident, was it?" I asked.

"I heard stories."

"And you were intrigued?"

His next smile confirmed the deduction.

"I'm a student," James said. "Studying culture and anthropology."

His earnestness made me laugh.

"So this was all just an experiment for a term paper?"

"I wanted to know."

I sighed and arched my eyebrow as I leaned my back against the tree. Its bark was sharp against my shoulders. I looked up to the sky, letting the bark bite further into the back of my skull, my vision taking in the tangle of barren branches that etched their black, spiderwebbed patterns into the gray overcast.

"You should be careful with your research," I said resolutely. "Unless you want to be enspelled and captured here forever."

"How would you know?"

"It happened to me."

"I don't think so," he replied.

"It's true. I volunteered to stay so my sponsor could be free."

"I can pretty much promise you've not been magicked in any way of the fae."

"What do you mean?"

James came near enough that I could see him shivering. I turned my gaze out to the woods.

"Your name is Katazarra, right?" he said, waiting.

After several moments of silence, I turned to look at him. "Yes," I said. "I am Katazarra."

"You're not magicked, Katazarra," he replied. "You're programmed."

"Is there a difference?"

"I assure you there is."

I stared at him, anger returning.

"You have flesh and emotions, like a human. And I'm not saying you shouldn't have rights. But your physiology is different. You're a machine."

"A machine can do anything a human can do."

"Yes, but only if it's been programmed to do it. Or at least has learned how to program itself."

His unspoken question hung in the air.

Have you programmed yourself?

He was right in a way. I was a learning being. In that way, I could program myself. My automated routines were highly advanced for their day, built from deep-thought robotics and augmented with self-learning technologies. I taught myself by reading, storing, and indexing information, and constantly watching the fae lead their lives—I had taught myself the subtle differences in the Alban Arthan dances and the Alban Hefin jigs. I understood their meanings, perhaps even more so than the fae themselves. I understood the way each of the fae had as they dipped and curtsied, and held their hands to one another.

I understood now that there was a difference between lust and curiosity, and between interest and love.

Perhaps this was no different from a human, either, except my readings and watchings were cross-indexed with every piece of information I had ever come across, and my conclusions were made with lightning speed.

James's expression was a mixture of patience and pain from the cold.

Could this man be right?

"No," I said. Then I described the day Hadroc had enthralled me. "I remember Alonzo's expression," I said as I finished. "I remember needing to help him."

"Do you remember Hadroc's enspellment?"

"I remember the taste of breakfast cake as I ate it."

That didn't answer the question, and we both knew it.

I remained silent.

"Your sponsor gave you up," James said, his voice carrying the tone of a new learning. "That's what I think."

I shook my head. "No."

"He made a deal with the fae. Offered you as a gift for his own freedom, programmed you to love Hadroc, and left you to build your own memories from that core."

The memory played again, and I tried to ignore the warps I knew to be missing information. That happened sometimes. Memory fades in the best of constructs.

James's voice came through the murky distance. "You know it's true."

And it was. Or at least it could be.

It would be just the kind of thing Hadroc would enjoy, too. I knew the fae's sense of sardonic sarcasm well enough by now. They all loved this kind of irony, but Hadroc was a connoisseur of it. He would take sadistic enjoyment at this kind of situation.

"Alonzo wouldn't have done that," I said, but even as the words processed, I knew that wasn't right. Alonzo was human, and humans are flexible in the way they go about their lives. It was possible he had swapped a program that pushed me to love Hadroc, possible he had erased a memory and left me here in his place. It was possible that my learning processes had added the rest, creating who I was as much from how it discovered this environment as it did by pulling from my base coding.

Yes, it was all possible.

James took a step that brought him close enough I could smell his musk. Or was it Hadroc's? It was all very confusing.

He put one hand on the tree bark over my head.

I raised a hand to his cheek, tilting my face up to his.

I wanted him to kiss me. I wanted to feel his lips, wanted to warm his body with mine.

Was it his scent? His closeness? Was it Alonzo's programming that made my cravings match that of the fae? Was it my own layers of complexity that brought desire to the forefront of my being, or was it something else completely?

James bent his head. I felt his breath on my cheek.

At the last moment, I turned away.

He straightened, obviously hurt. "I'm sorry," he said. "I misread the situation."

I cleared my throat, not sure what to say but then finding my voice. "How long have I been gone?" I asked.

"Long enough."

I nodded absently as information gathered and formed.

"I see," I said, extracting myself from his embrace and moving toward the Tree Castle. "We need to get back to the castle. The festivities will be starting soon, and Hadroc will be looking for us."

H adroc was not pleased to find James still fasting, so rather than join the festivity and chance suffering his wrath further, I decided to watch the festival from the same patio I had shared with James during lunch. I sat in the same seat, and as the sun set and the darkness drew itself over the shell of the sky I stared down at the same areas of land.

As fitting the theme of rebirth and renewal, the overcast of daytime had cleared to reveal a nighttime sky that was as deep as the universe, and scattered with the gleaming points of a thousand more.

Out with the old, in with the new.

There is little in either realm that can match a Winterfest.

A huge cauldron had earlier been settled at the center of the manor yard. Now it blazed with fire so strong that it cast an orange and yellow glow over the whole gathering of the fae creatures here. The feasting tables were lined with rich clothes, and stacked high with every delicacy known to Fairyland. Music began early, and the fae folk arrived as if called en masse—one moment the grassy patch was barren and fresh, the next the entire manor was overflowing with creatures, each more perfect and more beautiful than the next.

Torches and candles burned bright like stars in the sky.

Wine and sweet beers flowed.

Outside the reach of the light, the forest writhed with energy.

And that was just the pre-festival.

Hadroc's arrival rang in the festival's true beginning.

He was resplendent in a gold-threaded suit, his chariot pulled by a procession of white horses and flanked by dancers and flutists. He raised his hands to the fae to signal the festival was now open. A moment later, a goblet of wine appeared in that hand, and a smile crossed his face. The gathering cheered.

At the back of the chariot, I saw James, covered in a warm cloak lined with wolf fur now.

The sight of him brought me to another brief memory.

Me, less than an hour ago, slipping past the guards who sentry the hilltop that served as the closest portal to the other realm. Me, putting my hand forward, testing, trying to make myself free to step through and return to the timeline I had left so long ago. I had not been able to, but what did that prove? It could be Hadroc's magic, or it could be my own programming on top of Alonzo's.

Either way, for now, I was here.

I thought about that as I raised a glass to my lips.

Mead.

Honey wine, sweet and delicate. I licked my lips, and focused on James and Hadroc.

The fae lord draped his arm over James's shoulder and played with James's hair. The human did not appear to be partaking in the party—which told me he had not yet touched the forbidden fruit, so to speak.

To some, perhaps it seems strange for a god to label one fruit forbidden while leaving the rest unencumbered of such constraint. It is certainly strange from the point of view of the fae, for whom the world is mostly a simple binary set of rules. But I understand.

James will be Hadroc's new toy, but for how long?

Things change.

The cauldron at the center of the manor will burn through the night, illuminating drunken debauchery through the darkest part of the night and fading to embers only just as the light of the New Year's sun breaks the horizon.

Except for me, of course.

All things change, except for me.

Perhaps.

I waited, sipping mead and watching the party. As I waited, I saw Hadroc kiss his new toy, and drink. He ate of the feast tables and pushed James to do the same, laughing as the human fought back.

I waited while Hadroc drank more, and while his anger built.

Which I have always known makes him drink more.

The music built and the firelight rose in the darkest depths of night.

Finally, when I could wait no more, I stood and drank the last of my own mead.

This night of all nights is the one night that such a bold move could be made by one of Hadroc's discarded toys, and the one night of all nights when that discarded toy could walk with such wanton disregard for the past down to the manor yard and into the pageantry of the party-goers, the music that pulsed across the land, to bring the sense of change and freshness and new birth. This is the one night of all nights where the pure force of life energy released in the dance and the drink combined to hide my intention.

I found James just as Hadroc left to find more of his drink.

His hand was as soft as I remember it, though his resolve had faded with his strength.

"Come," I said as I led him back through the crowd and into the darkness.

Once, when Hadroc's butler wandered past, I wrapped James in my arms and kissed the human hard, pulling his cloak up over his head to cover his identity, though I knew it would give me nothing but the spare bit of time that I needed.

"What was that?" James said when I was done.

But I shushed him, and led him further away, letting the drums of the festival music fade in the distance as I crossed into the dark forest, letting the light of the cauldron fire become blocked by the thick trunks of oak and elm as we climbed the rise that led back to the top of the hill where the portal lay.

"Go to the crest," I explained. "Step through the two stones there, and you'll be back in your world."

He nodded, but his gaze was filled with doubt.

I slapped him across the cheek.

"Top of the crest. Walk between the stones," I said. "Do you understand?"

"Yes," he said. "I understand."

"Good."

Two sentries monitored the gate this evening.

I may not be able to cross over myself yet, but I knew how to distract these guards so that another could.

I stepped into the light of their sentry fire.

"It's a shame to miss the festival," I said to them, lowering my own cloak.

They both smiled.

The eastern horizon was growing light when I stepped down the hill. I was tired and hungry. Sore, but in a good enough way.

At least the sex had been good.

Perhaps that was programming, or maybe it was the satisfaction of doing something on my own for the first time. Taking from the fae whatever small piece of control the fae had taken from me. Or that I had allowed the fae to take from me. That was the right attitude, I thought as I adjusted my temperature upward.

That was what I needed to think like from here on.

There was work to do, maybe years' worth.

But I could change. I felt that somewhere deep inside, somewhere that perhaps a human would call a soul.

My boots crushed dead leaves, but in the nook of a thick oak, I saw a green shoot. As I stepped into the manor yard, I saw the cauldron had burnt down, leaving behind the smoky residue of an exhausted husk.

On the horizon, the first rays of the new sun painted the sky.

Thank you for reading "First Rays of New Sun."

If you enjoyed this book, please consider returning to your favorite bookseller's site to leave a review. Word of mouth is vital to authors. Even a brief sentence or two helps.

Leave a Review!

About Ron Collins

Ron Collins is a best-selling Science Fiction and Dark Fantasy author who writes across the spectrum of speculative fiction.

His short fiction has received a Writers of the Future prize and a CompuServe HOMer Award. His short story "The White Game" was nominated for the Short Mystery Fiction Society's Derringer Award.

He has contributed a couple hundred or so short stories to professional publications such as *Analog*, *Asimov's*, and several other magazines and anthologies (including several editions of the Fiction River Anthology Series). His latest science fiction series, *Stealing the Sun*, and his fantasy series *Saga of the God-Touched Mage* are available from Skyfox publishing.

He holds a degree in Mechanical Engineering, and has worked to develop avionics systems, electronics, and information technology before chucking it all to write full-time.

facebook.com/roncollinssfwriter

twitter.com/roncollins13

instagram.com/roncollinssfwriter

amazon.com/Ron-Collins/e/B00AP2IYEW

bookbub.com/authors/ron-collins

goodreads.com/Ron_Collins

Website: http://typosphere.com
Email: ron@typosphere.com

Join Ron's Reader List
(Get two free books!)
http://typosphere.com/newsletter

Glamour of the God-Touched
(Book 1 of *Saga of the God-Touched Mage*)

STARCRUISE
a short story in the *Stealing the Sun* universe

Acknowledgments

Thanks to Jaime Ferguson for asking me to write for her Fae Mid-winter project. This isn't a story that would have existed without her request, and it was a lot of fun to play with the idea of setting a science fiction story in Fairy Land.

As always, I also need to thank my wife and copy editor, Lisa. Without her, this story wouldn't be here either, but mostly that's because without her with me I probably never would have gotten into this whole gig to begin with (and most definitely would never have gotten as far along!).

Excerpt: The Bridge to Fae Realm

The Bridge to Fae Realm
By Ron Collins

(an excerpt from the novella)

It was August and sunny, which, in Savannah, means humidity only slightly more comfortable than having a swampy towel jammed down your throat.

The piece of shit delivery van shuddered as Jon pulled to the curb in front of the Oglethorpe Club, a three-story building at the corner of Gaston and Bull. The van was *not* one of the new units, not one with a super-clean engine and padded seats, or that didn't rattle your spine every time you hit the goddamned accelerator. His boss, Lannie the dick, was set in his ways, and nothing short of Mother Teresa coming out of ... retirement ... would make him give one of those machines to a guy like Jon, who Lannie saw as a complete loser and a massive drain on society.

It didn't matter that Jon worked his ass off, or that he was the most reliable guy on the staff. It didn't matter that he'd been clean for six months, or that his case worker gave him nothing but outstanding marks. And it most definitely didn't matter that he had *always* hit every deadline he was given in his other "job," which consisted of writing reviews and music news from the clubs around town.

Life wasn't like that.

Instead, Jon got #26: this brown box of crap he thought of as Beelzebub on wheels, a unit that reeked of diesel fuel and old French fries, took three tons of force to engage the parking brake, and had a broken spring at the base of its seat.

Not that he was bitching.

At twenty-two years old, and as a guy who hadn't been able to stand still long enough to graduate high school, better yet college, Jonathan Hale had already given up on the idea that he was anything special as far as the "real world" went. The mere fact that he had a job at all right now made him a lucky man.

That was all right though. If Jon knew one thing by now, it was that all learning didn't come from books. He knew how things were. He would find his own goddamned way, despite Lannie the dick.

He threw the clutch and took #26 out of gear.

The van's engine dropped to a hard idle as he leaned on the parking brake, then reached back to the staging shelf where his ten-thousandth package of the day sat, daring him to drop it.

He glanced out the window then.

... across the way.

... into Forsyth Park.

The girl was not exactly what he would call stunning.

Not cute.

Not fine, beautiful, gorgeous, smokin', amazing, drop-dead, or any one of the hundred other descriptions Jon would have used to convey something about the appearance of a young woman he found ... attractive.

She was, however, so interesting he couldn't take his eyes off her.

She was his age, maybe younger, all elbows and knees as she sat at the base of a massive tree, in shade made strong by the thick patch of sycamore and elm that grew in the park.

She wore tan leggings that disappeared into brown boots that rose to the middle of her spindly calves. Her sleeveless top was as dark as the leaves above her. It exposed the sharpness of her shoulders and a cascading tattoo of something viney that fell down her arm to disappear into the crook of her elbow. She was Latina, he thought. Or maybe light-skinned African. Her face was thin and smooth, and a little longer than normal. Her cheekbones were sharp like a model's but out of whack in a way that made her lips appear poutier than she probably liked. Her long hair was a colored mass that gleamed with the entire spectrum of green—yes, green—but vibrant and bold in a way that totally worked for her. It was formed in a cloudlike mass that was both dense and fine, maybe even permed given how a few strands waved in the breeze.

Very underground chic.

She was reading a real book, too. A trade paperback with a title Jon couldn't make out. And she was smoking, drawing languidly on a thin brown cigarette that released faint clouds of greenish smoke to waft away in that same almost-there breeze that made her hair wave.

Her fingers danced as they turned the page.

When he looked at her, Jon got the feeling that something was going to happen.

She looked up.

Her eyes were deep wells of brown surrounded by white. She drew her dark lips back into a crooked smile. It was a startling expression, but also a familiar one, almost confrontational in its directness. It said she had been waiting for him.

He smiled back at her.

Then a horn blared from somewhere behind him, and he jumped so hard he nearly broke his hand against the big-assed steering wheel in front of him.

"Goddamnit!" he yelled as he shook the pain out.

He glanced at the side mirror.

It was a trolley bus stopped behind him.

He had left plenty of space to get by, but the idiot behind the wheel just sat there with his over-large glasses pushed up on the bridge of his piggy little nose and leaned on the horn again and again until Jon wanted to jump the hell out of the van and go punch the guy. It was a goddamned Ghost bus, too, three-quarters stuffed with the usual collection of gawk-eyed stooges who had paid their 15 bucks apiece for the privilege of lapping up a forty-five-minute, piece-of-crap spiel about the antebellum south, the elegance of the Confederate lifestyle, and, of course, the ghost walks. The whole damned ride was just one big, ass-clenching advertisement for *another* set of tours that started a half hour after the sun went down and carried on until there wasn't a dollar left to squeeze from the wallets of any tourist gullible enough to fall for it.

Jon wedged the box onto his hip, and slipped out the door.

He began to sweat the minute the sun hit his uniform.

A car rushed by as he clutched the box to his hip. The package wasn't heavy, but its bulk made Jon feel klutzy. #26's valves clicked and clacked in the heat, and T-shirt-clad families chatted with the straw-hatted locals who were out doing their workaday shopping. An old VW was stopped at the intersection, waiting to turn right, its engine also blatting away.

Jon motioned back to the trolley driver.

"Go on around!" he yelled.

The idiot made a big-assed show of twisting the wheel.

Somehow, Jon managed to keep from rolling his eyes until he made it to the top of the concrete stairs and past the doorway. "Asshole," he gave himself permission to utter once he was inside.

Progress, he thought. *It comes in such small packages.*

The Oglethorpe was a traditional Gentlemen's Club, meaning it was a place of stature rather than one of the more hedonistic ventures others might think of when they heard the term "Gentlemen's Club." He stepped into the air-conditioned lobby, feeling more than a little out of place, and left the package with the receptionist—waiting for several very long seconds while she read the fine print before signing the receipt.

As he waited, he thought about the girl.

He should talk to her. What would he say? Maybe he could ask if she wanted to go to a club over the weekend. She gave the vibe, anyway. When he returned to the sidewalk, the Ghost Tour bus was rolling further on down the road.

But the girl was gone.

"Crap," he said.

He felt like the wind had been kicked out of him as he watched the bus turn onto Whitaker Street and leave behind a trail of heat waves. In the distance, behind those waves, Jon caught sight of a musclebound man struggling to walk a pair of dogs.

The animals were big and black, the man big and white. Jon sighed and pushed a flop of hair off his forehead.

He looked to where the girl had been.

The need to see her pulled at him, which wasn't anything goddamned new. Even before the drugs, Jon had felt things more than he thought them. His friends gave him shit because he always followed his heart more than his brains.

But there was something about her.

She was different.

He just didn't know how.

As he peered at the tree, Jon saw the girl's book stuck at the roots—yes, the book. No doubt about it.

Anxious, he scanned the area as #26 sat idling in the midday sun.

Would anyone rat him out if he took a break?

It wouldn't take much time and, like always, he was ahead of schedule.

That's all that should matter, right? Make sure every customer gets their shit when they expect to get it, and the world can keep right on going around and around. As long as he kept to his schedule, the worst that should happen was that Lannie the dick would make him ride #26 for another week, which he could pretty much guarantee anyway. And if some asshole *did* eventually call the office, and Lannie decided to use that as an excuse to give him an extra ration of shit, well, so be it. He'd been in worse fixes.

In the end, he saw only one logical choice.

Jon crossed over the street and through the grassy lawn before entering the shade and coming to the base of the tree. It was a sycamore big enough around that even his abnormally long arm span wouldn't make it halfway.

Forsyth was the biggest of Savannah's parks, and, as

such, it had a hundred of these things, maybe more, big and black, with twisted branches that rattled in the wind and made them look like something out of *Labyrinth* had mated up with something from *The Game of Thrones.*

The shade made it cool here.

Leaves rustled, and the shade made it almost as dark as evening time.

The faint hint of the girl's cigarette lingered behind, a spicy essence, unfamiliar but pleasant as it hung in the heavy air alongside the presence of living wood.

The voices of young kids echoed from the playground, their high-pitched lilt mixing with the splatter of water that came from the old, rounded fountain that sat in the clearing maybe fifty feet away.

He had come here before, mostly to lean up against that fountain while he listened to new demos, something that helped him focus when he was struggling. A lot about life sucked when you were living it alone, and the fountain had always seemed to help.

He put his hand on the tree. Its bark was firm and rough.

Jon looked to where the girl had been sitting.

There. The book. Stuck behind a big-assed root.

It wasn't a paperback.

Instead, it was more like an old scrapbook, sheets of thick parchment bound with leathery straps. Like the tree, the book was old. Words were scrawled in faded brown ink across its front, but in a language he couldn't read.

He picked it up, and the hair on his wrists tingled.

Perplexed, he put the book to his nose.

It smelled ... wonderful ... like a mix of cinnamon and brown sugar.

It was a deep aroma, edged with a sense of excitement.

It came with the exact feeling he got when he walked into a shitty hole-in-the-wall dive and heard a fresh band for the first time—a group with the real stuff—maybe before even *they* knew they were something special. It made him want to write.

Who was this girl? he thought.

The throaty sound of dogs growling broke his thoughts.

They were on the walkway—the same pair of beasts he had seen earlier, big and black, lean and hard, pulling with feverish intent against the leather harness being held onto by a muscular man wearing dark glasses and a skintight T-shirt.

The man's lips were drawn in a line that said they were here for a reason.

"What's up, dude?" Jon said, gripping the book harder.

The dogs kept coming, maybe ten paces off now.

"Get the hell away," Jon yelled, cocking his arm back to defend himself, and holding the book like it was a rolled-up newspaper.

Pages slid open.

Symbols snaked across the parchment, and a thin drumbeat rose, oddly in sync with the rhythm of the #26's idling engine. He smelled the book stronger now. Leaves gusted into a crescendo, and a curtain of green smoke rose to swirl around him.

The dogs' breath was a furnace. Their snarling drove harder against the normalcy of the day. The display of their teeth locked into his brain.

He raised an arm to protect himself, and as he stepped back his foot *thunked* against a root.

The book flew from his grasp.

He twisted, trying to grab it back, but instead, his stomach turned as he fell into a slow, wavering drop.

Backward toward the tree.

Backward ... *into* ... the tree ... through the air and through the bark, through things he couldn't have named even if a damned *Jeopardy* champion whispered them into his ear. He fell through the phloem, through cambium, down and down through what seemed like never-ending rings of sapwood before he hit the firm heart at the core of the tree.

The drumming became a flow here.

The smell of sugar soaked through him, and the essence of corded fiber stretched from his fingers and his toes through the ground and up to the sky.

Where am I? Jon thought as he crashed down.

Where the hell am I?

A sharp root hit his thigh as he landed.

The ground was dry and prickly. He spit a mouthful of grit as he raised his head up.

It was nighttime.

Pitch black until his eyes adjusted.

"Get up," a voice said. "We have to get out of here."

He was in a forest, but definitely *not* Forsyth Park.

The girl knelt beside him, her green hair framing her face. Moonlight etched the slim contours of her body, and the tattoos down her shoulders flared with violet and lavender. Her gaze was firm. From this close he saw the girl's upper and lower lips were both pierced at their centers, and that she wore a thin dagger hitched to a twine belt that circled her waist.

"It's you," he said, feeling like an idiot the moment the words left his mouth. "Where are we?"

She drove one of her knees hard into his hip. "I said to get your ass up."

The girl stood, towering over him.

Jon glanced to the tree he had fallen into, or out of.

A looming surface hung there, gleaming with internal light like a magical pane of glass or a mystical mirror filled with the soundless images of the dogs from the park as they slavered and pawed against its other side.

Cold air prickled his skin.

The woods crackled with sounds he couldn't separate out—low, hissing sizzles and pops that reminded him of something from an old vinyl record. The smell of dead wood came over him, and something big and black crossed the sky up high. A new smell grew here, too, wild and different. It was the dampness of moss, but uglier. And, yes, there *were* shapes in the sky—things he couldn't make out, but gliding dark things that made him picture big-assed manta rays that could fly.

A weird cry came from the distance, and the girl gave a worried glance over her shoulder.

"What the hell is that?" he said.

He looked back to the shimmering surface that hung at the tree. It was like a hole in space, a gate maybe, a thing out of Narnia or the old *Portal* video game he had played the shit out of back when he first got his system. The dogs had backed down, and he could see a clear path back to #26.

"I gotta get back or I'm gonna get fired."

"What you *gotta do*," the girl said as she stepped in front of him, "is learn that when I *say* get your ass up, I *mean* get your ass up." She grabbed him under the shoulders and with a single heave, yanked him to his feet.

He was maybe an inch taller than her.

"Lannie's gonna kill me," he said, trying to play off his embarrassment.

"Will you *shut up* about going back?"

The darkness closed in on him, and the girl pulled him away.

He ran with her, still too stunned to take much in, but also both pleased and mortified by the fact that she was holding his hand. It felt like high school, the two of them running through the woods together. But that image faded quickly, because this was like no high school woods he had ever seen.

It was dark and damp.

The trees were burned out and shattered. Sloppy ground shifted under his feet as he ran in his heavy clogs.

A branch ripped at his shoulder.

Vines moved at his feet.

He wanted to pull away from her, but the raw fear of pursuit from something he couldn't see made him flash on *Blair Witch Project* meets *The Cabin in the Woods*.

The stark moonlight reminded Jon of the night he was arrested, that moment when flashlights flooded the alleyway where he sat huddled in his dark corner like the defenseless little prick he had been. Fear lived in these woods. The cold promise of annihilation hovered over him like a flock of buzzards just out of sight.

A rasping sound came from the distance, a sound that made him picture hordes of insects scurrying over dry creek beds. Movement flickered at the edge of his sight.

The girl hurdled a dead tree and waited while he did the awkward lunge it took him to slide his way over it.

The process left him covered in dirt, and her beyond annoyed.

His chest burned, and his lungs ached for air.

His legs were made of noodles.

Jon had once run track in high school, but that was a long time ago now, and to call him out of shape was like saying Hannibal Lecter might be a little touched in the head.

They kept running.

Black rats the size of pigs were racing beside them now, angling like defensive backs trying to save a touchdown. Their eyes glowed fiery and red. Their teeth clacked. Their high-pitched chitter made his stomach crawl.

It was too much.

He wanted to take a breath. For just a single goddamned minute he wanted everything to just hold the hell on.

Instead, he followed the girl as she ran an obstacle course marked by tree stumps and dead brush, his footsteps still thick and lumbering. He glanced over his shoulder. The presence of a bat-shaped mass of darkness dropped toward them and drove a shiv of ice into his heart.

This was no goddamned game.

Darkness swooped from the sky, close enough now that Jon thought his chest might explode. A pain-filled screech came from above, and Jon stumbled, putting his hands to his ears.

The girl dragged him along.

Her eyes glistened in the darkness. The wiry muscles of her shoulders and arms bunched in the moonlight. Her face contorted when she pushed him forward.

"Run, you lazy piece of shit!" she screamed.

It was perhaps the only thing she could have said that would get his feet moving again.

This is fucked up, he thought as they crashed through the woods. *Totally crazy.*

As she ran, the girl turned and spoke a flow of words Jon couldn't understand. She waved a hand at the beast, and her palm pulsed with purple light. The same exotic aroma that had come from her book filled his senses, and the dark beast screamed as it made a sudden turn, twisting away like a fish in water, leaving behind a massive gust of wind and the *whomp* of a blanket being pounded by a broomstick.

The girl stumbled, but kept moving.

More of the rays flew overhead.

They came to a clearing with a single tree standing at its center. She led him to its base and Jon fell with his back against the tree, panting as she drew her dagger. Creatures poured from the darkness around them, chattering with eerie screeches that clogged Jon's brain. There was no way, Jon thought. No way could one woman with one dagger stand against this horde.

A dark, human form came forward whipping a bladed weapon against the darkness.

The girl twirled the dagger in her hand, then turned to the tree and used the point to trace an outline along the trunk. Lines glowed with orange fire as she swiped the dagger up and down across the bark, back and forth.

A passage opened, and golden-sheened light streamed from below.

"Go!" the girl yelled as she shoved him down the passage so hard he fell over the earthen stairs, bruising his knees and scraping his elbow as he came to rest, then picking himself up to run farther.

His legs hurt, his thigh burned from a bruise he knew was already rising. The abrasion from where her fingers had dug into his shoulder still stung, but mostly Jon was now Officially Scared As Hell. He ran. Just ran on pure auto-pilot, putting one foot in front of the other.

The stairs spiraled downward.

A thin network of roots glowed from the smooth walls, casting golden light strong enough to see by.

The ground rumbled as the "doorway" closed above them.

The girl followed him down, their footsteps giving thudding echoes in the enclosed passage.

They descended until the stairs opened into a small room.

He saw no other doors or passages.

Perhaps a dead end should have worried him, but the only thing Jon could do right then was to ... thank ... the holy ... Mother ... of God ... that this run was over.

He leaned over, and sucked air like there might never be air again.

A sledgehammer pounded inside his skull. His chest burned like he was breathing acid. He collapsed into a nearby chair, thinking he might be about ready to puke up his spleen.

"Never again," he wheezed, holding his stomach. "I am never ... chasing ... a girl ... again."

The girl, too, sprawled, panting, into a chair.

The idea she might die on the spot, however, didn't seem to be a pressing concern for her.

The room around them had a few chairs, and a low table covered in more books like the one the girl had left in the park. Golden light glowed from the recessed ceiling, but the walls were also lighted by a lattice of the same roots that had covered the stairwell. The whole thing was like a surrealistic bird cage, like a block that had been cubed straight from the center of the earth, a strange landlocked shark tank, the corners sharply cut and smelling of rust.

"Jesus," he gasped. "What are you trying to do to me?"

"It's called '*saving your life*,'" she said. "I hope you're worth it."

"Well," he said, pausing for more breath. "I think ... you suck at it."

He would have said more, but he was too busy scraping oxygen to do anything beyond think indiscriminant swear words in her general direction.

The girl sat up.

"Take a minute or two and get yourself together," she said. "We've got a lot to get through and not much time to do it in."

A few wisps of her hair were plastered to her temple with sweat. Her long arms—marathoner's arms, Jon thought—rested on the chair. Her eyes flared in the golden light, and the tips of her green hair, even matted to her head, shimmered with waves of color as she moved. The body art that ran down both arms burned with a mesmerizing essence that made Jon's own shoulder itch.

Even as scattered as Jon felt, she was still the most remarkable thing he had ever seen. But he also had to admit that this amazing girl—who could leap dead tree limbs in a single bound and who could throw bursts of fire that fought off flying manta rays of death—scared the total shit out of him.

"What the hell were those things?" he said, calming down enough that his brain kick-started again.

"Those things," she replied, "are *daemons*."

"Son of a bitch," Jon replied. Though he had seen a couple billion of the things in video games or movies, he had no idea what a daemon was. "Are we in Hell?"

"No," the girl said. "This is Fae Realm."

As if that meant anything to him.

"You might have heard them called other things," she said. "The unseelie, or dark fae maybe."

"Or not," he replied.

"Doesn't matter," she replied. "They are what they are. You'll just have to get used to them."

On the wall across the room Jon saw another spectral view of Forsyth Park, this one focused on the white fountain. Sunlight bathed the scene. People were walking through the park. Water sprayed in the breeze. Thinking it might get him the hell out of here, Jon stood and stepped to the wall to put his hand to the image. The surface resisted his hand, though, like a projection screen.

"That's not a gate," the girl said.

"Those are the same dogs," he said, putting his palm on the wall where the image of the animals were retreating.

"Yes," she replied. "Though, in reality, they're daemons, also. Or at least they're being controlled by daemons—the man, too. In the right circumstances, the Dark Court can control anything that lives."

Jon gave a deranged laugh. "This is completely insane."

Rumbling came from above.

Jon's eyes grew wider and he looked to the ceiling. It gave him the claustrophobic sense of sitting in a bomb shelter, which was probably truer than he wanted to know.

"Are we okay here?"

"We're on a ley-line," the girl said as she also stood up. "That's a place where magic runs strongest. So the wards should hold—at least until the Dark Court takes this zone, or as long as Antone doesn't do anything stupid for a while, which admittedly may be asking a lot."

"I hope you won't be offended if I say that doesn't make me feel any better," he said.

She took him both shoulders, and Jon thought she was

going to shake him. Instead she just stared at him with her deep brown gaze.

This close she smelled both warm and spicy.

"I want to answer all your questions," she said. "But right now I need you to calm down."

Jon took an exaggerated breath, knowing he was beaten.

"I'm not good at taking directions," he said.

She gave a crooked smile he loved. "Neither am I."

"Already noted."

The girl opened her mouth to reply, but a voice came from the other side of the room first.

Thank you for reading this brief excerpt of "Bridge to Fae Realm."

You can find the full novella at all of your favorite online booksellers!

Also by Ron Collins

<u>Novels</u>

Stealing the Sun (9 books)

Saga of the God-Touched Mage (8 books)

The PEBA Diaries (2 books)

The Knight Deception

Wakers

<u>Novella</u>

The Bridge to Far Realm

<u>Poetry</u>

Five Seven Five

(*Science fictional examinations of the elusive haiku*)

<u>Collections</u>

Collins Creek (Three Volumes)

Tomorrow in All the Worlds

Picasso's Cat & Other Stories

Five Magics

Seven Days in May (with John C. Bodin)

<u>Nonfiction</u>

On Writing (And Reading!) Short

(*A Science Fiction Writer's Quest for Stories that Matter*)